I
HATE
TO GO
TO BED

I HATE TO GO TO BED

by Judi Barrett

Illustrated by Ray Cruz

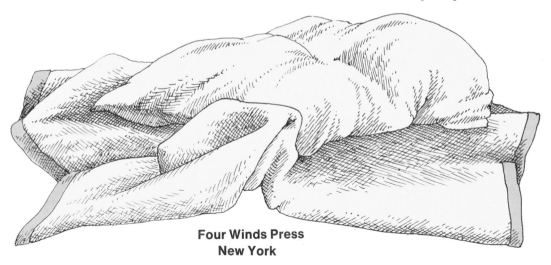

Four Winds Press
New York

LIBRARY OF CONGRESS CATALOGING IN PUBLICATION DATA
Barrett, Judith.
I hate to go to bed.
SUMMARY: A youngster lists all the pleasant and
unpleasant things about going to bed.
[1. Sleep—Fiction]   I. Cruz, Ray.   II. Title.
PZ7.B27521ad   [E]   77–1583
ISBN 0–590–07472–5

Published by Four Winds Press
A Division of Scholastic Magazines, Inc., New York, N.Y.
Text copyright © 1977 by Judi Barrett
Illustrations copyright © 1977 by Ray Cruz
Printed in the United States of America
Library of Congress Catalog Card Number: 77–1583

1 2 3 4 5   81 80 79 78 77

I
HATE
TO GO
TO BED
BECAUSE

My parents say I have to.

I'm still wide awake and not sleepy at all.

I'm the youngest and I have to go to bed first.

I have to stop having fun and put all my toys away.

I have to get out of all my clothes
and into my pajamas.

I have to brush my teeth with gooey toothpaste.

My sheets feel awfully cold when I crawl into them.

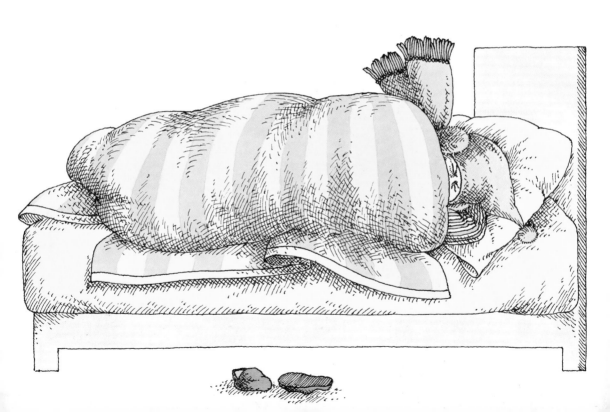

Everyone else is still awake watching television.

It's kind of dark in my room.

I imagine there might be monsters hiding in the corners.

And, sometimes I feel like I'm all alone lying there.

BUT
IF I
HAVE TO
GO
TO BED

I can stay up a few minutes longer sipping warm cocoa.

I can wear my number 25 football pajamas.

All my stuffed animal friends are waiting for me there.

I can read under the covers.

I can snuggle deep down into the bottom of my pillow.

My bed gets all soft and warm after I'm in it.

I can talk to myself about secret things
and no one will hear.

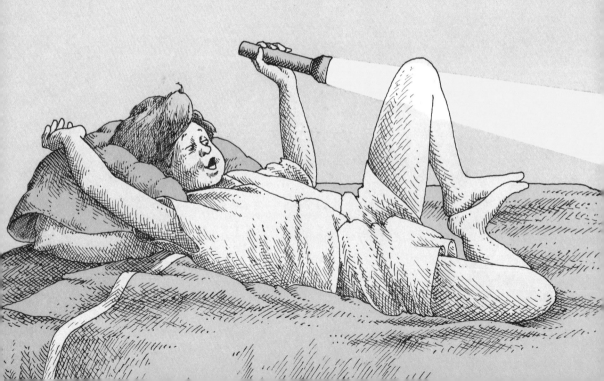

I can shine my flashlight through the darkness.

I can shoot any monsters dead with my ray gun.

Sometimes I can touch the moonlight
coming through my window.

I can sleep under my favorite old baby blanket.

I might even go on a dangerous
African safari in my dreams.

And, I can get dressed
under the covers on cold mornings.

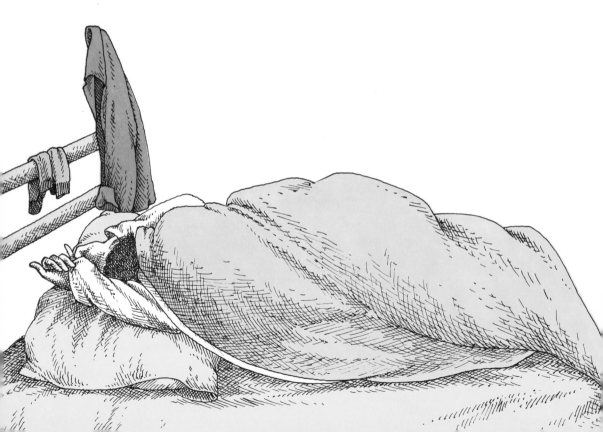

I think what I hate most about going to bed at night is that I have to get up in the morning.